NO KKN

M IS FOR MOVEMENT

AKA HUMANS CAN'T EAT GOLF BALLS

By Innosanto Nagara

New York • Oakland • London

1

MONSOON BORN

I was born in the eye of a Monsoon Storm.

The storm had been pounding the island for days. My parents lived in a small house in a *kampung* on the island of Java. *Kampung* means "village," from a long time ago when you had to walk through forests and rice paddies to get from one to the next. Back then each kampung was part of a kingdom, and there were many kingdoms here.

The kings were always wanting more power, and sometimes they would go to war with each other. The villagers were always caught in the middle. They would pretend they loved their king and hated the king next door. But all the kings took their rice and made their young boys fight and kill and die in their wars. The villagers didn't really care which king was their king. Everyone except for the royal family hated the king.

Our island may not be what you think of when you think of an island. For one thing, it's huge. It takes three days to drive from one end to the other. Over the years, the kampungs grew into cities, the cities into big cities, and the big cities into one huge metropolis. There are no longer any rice paddies left around my kampung. Just houses and streets and more houses and more streets. By the time I was born, TEN MILLION people lived in my city.

My kampung is called Menteng. My city: Jakarta, the capital of Indonesia. There are SEVENTEEN THOUSAND islands in my country—it is a land of islands. So many that you can't see them all on a map. There are even islands where real-life dragons still live. Look up "Komodo dragons" if you don't believe me.

On Java, it wasn't unusual to have storms that time of year. It was monsoon season! But this storm came during another kind of storm, a political storm—a time when people were clashing over who should rule the country. A time of turmoil.

I was just being born, so I didn't care about any of that. And my parents, who usually cared a lot about what was going on in the country, that night only cared about me being born.

The storm raged for days, and many parts of the city were flooded.

We were lucky that Menteng was on a bit of a hill, so our house was wet but not underwater. Still, nobody could go anywhere. The water was rushing through our streets like a raging river. Our electricity had been out for days, so my parents lit a kerosene lamp for light. The wind was howling and whistling through the windows; the lamp was flickering like it was going to go out any moment. Flashes of lightning lit up the sky, followed almost immediately by deep, rumbling thunder. Nobody was going out in that storm, not even to have a baby.

Then, almost suddenly, the whistling of the wind stopped, and the pounding of the rain on the roof died down. You could still hear the storm rumbling off in the distance, and there was a light pitter-patter of small raindrops hitting the windows, but otherwise all was still . . . all was quiet.

It was the eye of the storm.

It was then that I let out my first howl, and the whole kampung knew I was born.

***

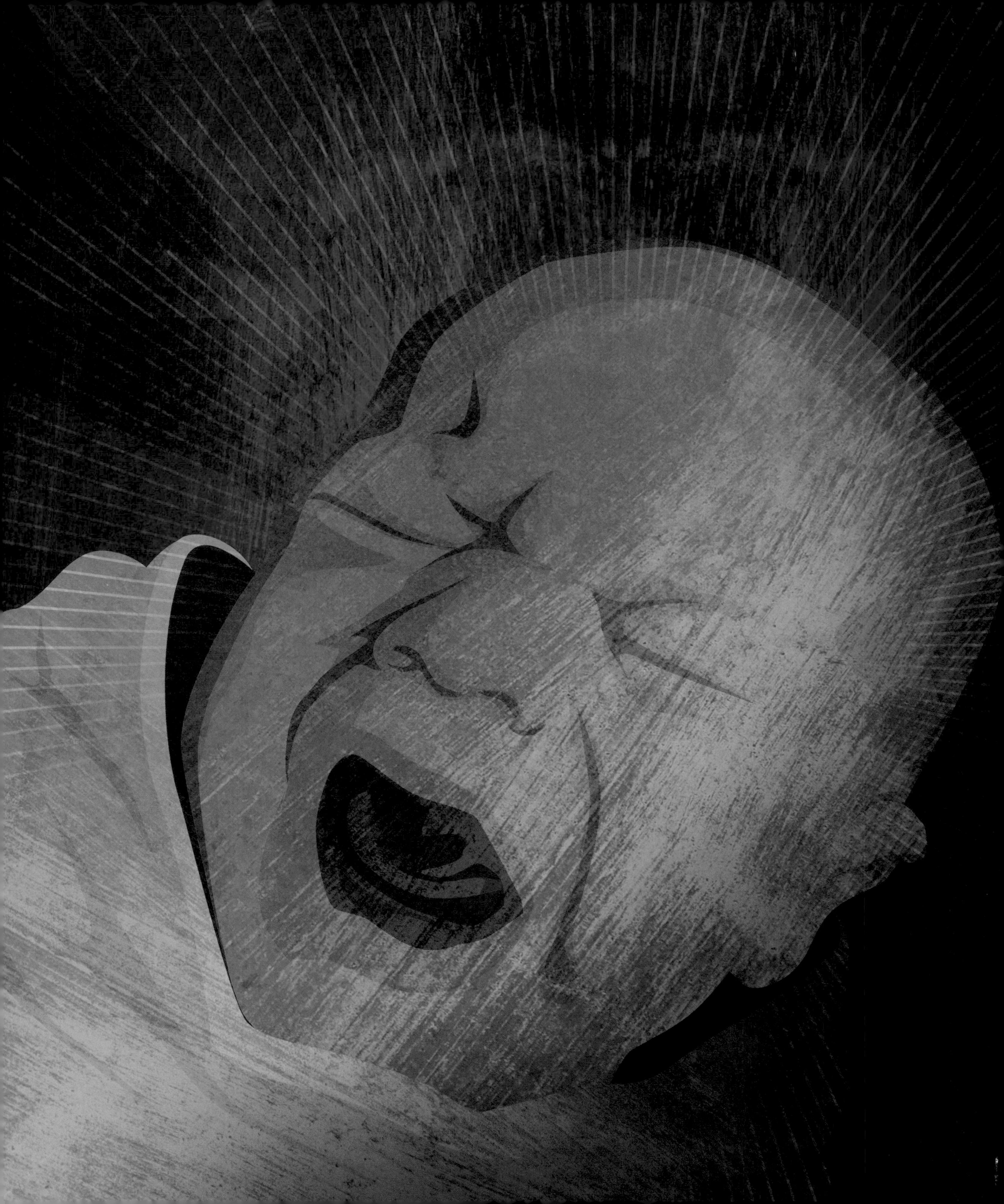

By the way, I think I forgot to mention to you that while this may feel like a true story, not everything in it is exactly True. Some of it happened. Some of it could have happened. Some of it happened to me and some to other people. Some of it may never have happened at all—at least not exactly in the way I'm telling this story.

But I'm not making this all up out of nowhere. What I'm telling you about is real. Stories can be real even if they're not true stories.

Are you okay with that? Good. I'll go on now.

***

Soon the eye of the storm passed, and our kampung was pounded by the rain and wind and thunder and lightning again. My family hunkered down until it passed. And after it did, there I was, the new baby in kampung Menteng.

When the roads were cleared, our friends and relatives came to visit. They brought food for my parents and gifts for the new baby. They tickled my toes and pinched my cheeks and made silly sounds that grown-ups like to make to babies to freak them out . . . I mean, to get them to laugh. Since I was the first child born to anyone in my parents' group of friends, and I was the first grandchild in our family, everyone was really excited that I had been born.

Everyone, that is, except for the Minister.

This government minister was an important person in Indonesia. He was just one step down from the president, and pretty much nothing happened without his permission. So everyone tried to be on his good side, even when they didn't like him.

My parents brought me to visit the Minister, since that's what you did. When you're a new baby, everyone who really cares about you visits. And people like the Minister expect your parents to bring you to them. Of course he said all the nice things people say when they are introduced to a new baby.

Being a baby, I just did what babies do: I spit up on him. He wasn't pleased about that. But it was nothing personal. I spit up on a lot of people back then. I spit up on people I liked too, like my parents and my other baby friends. Spit-up wasn't even the grossest thing that people had to deal with when taking care of me as a baby.

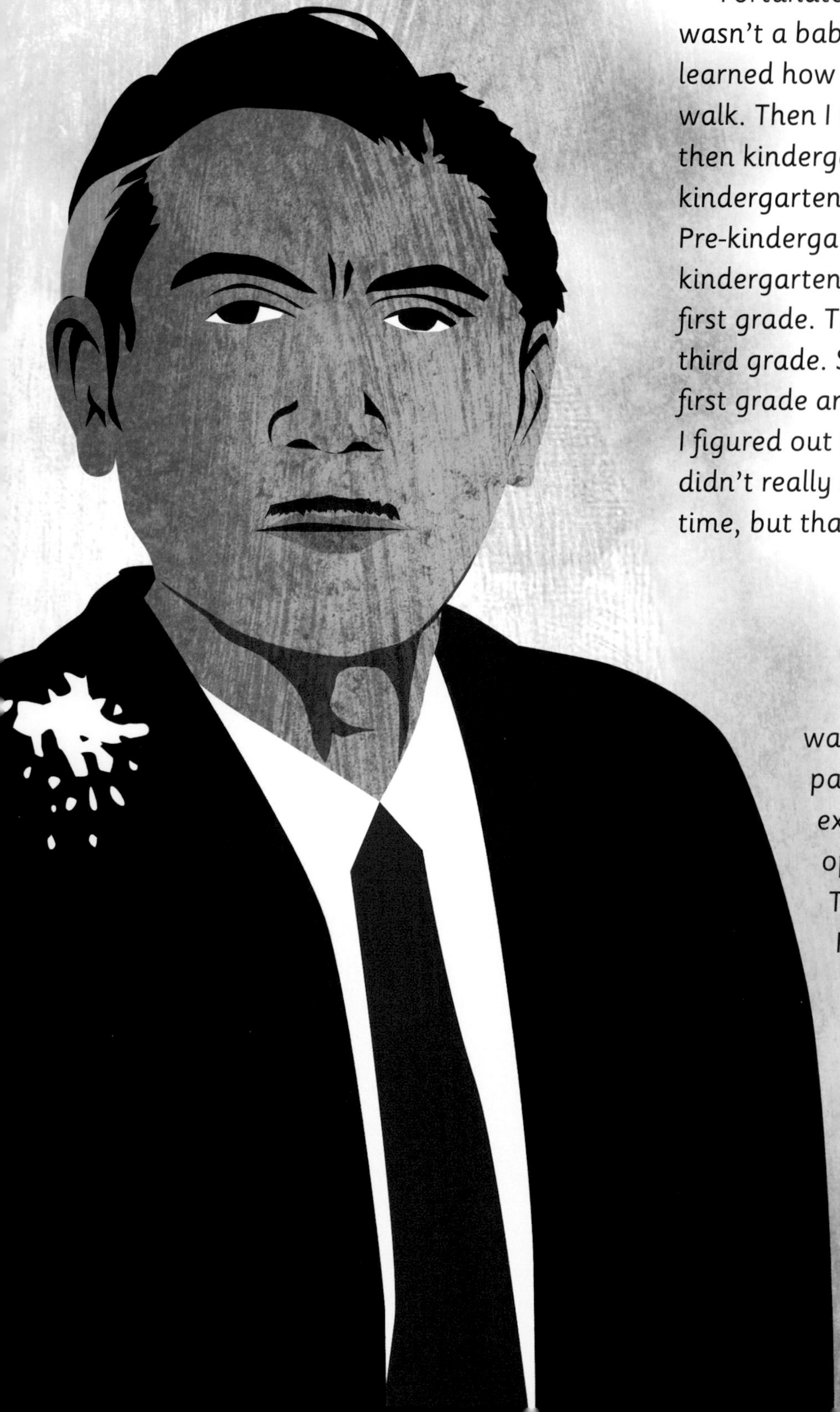

Fortunately for everyone, I wasn't a baby forever. I eventually learned how to toddle. Then to walk. Then I went to preschool. And then kindergarten. In Indonesia, kindergarten is called grade zero. Pre-kindergarten was "little zero" and kindergarten was "big zero." Then first grade. Then second grade. Then third grade. Somewhere between first grade and third grade is when I figured out I had a superpower. I didn't really see it that way at the time, but that's how I see it now.

***

To start with, my family was different because my parents were born on the exact same day, but on opposite sides of the earth. The earth is TWENTY-FOUR THOUSAND miles all the way around. My dad was born almost exactly halfway across the world from where my mom was born.

Of course I'm not the only kid with parents who come from halfway around the world from each other. And even people who grow up across the street from each other can be very different. But when I was a kid, having parents who were so different from each other made me different. Being different sometimes made me feel special, which was good. Sometimes it made me feel I didn't fit in, which was awkward. I spent a lot of time trying to fit in.

I also felt different because a lot of people knew who my father was. Wherever I went, people would say, "Oh, you're *his* kid!" People knew who he was because he was a *dissident*. That means when he didn't agree with the people in power, he said so. He registered his *dissent*. He wrote articles and books that told the truth about what some people in the government were doing. People like the Minister, as I discovered later. Sometimes his books were banned. Which means bookstores weren't allowed to sell them, and if you owned a copy you had to throw it away or you could get into trouble. Free speech was not a right.

What that meant for me was that if I did anything I wasn't supposed to do and people saw me, they'd know who I was and they'd tell my parents and I'd get in trouble. Or worse, my parents would get in trouble. Having people you care about get into trouble because of something you did is even worse than getting in trouble yourself.

I learned THAT the hard way.

2

PANZERS

My friend and I were just being curious.

Our school was a long way from my house. It took about an hour to get there every day, and another hour to get back home. I had to get up at five in the morning to get to school before the bell rang at six fifty. Yup. School started at seven in the morning when I was a kid.

After school I would just hang out until I got picked up—which was sometimes pretty late in the day since my parents were busy at work and traffic was always bad in Jakarta.

My school was right next to a university, and one day on the way to school I saw a line of tanks surrounding the university. These were small tanks called panzers. My mom explained to me that the panzers were there because the university students had been holding protests against the government, and the army was trying to scare the students into not protesting. As a kid, I didn't pay that much attention to what was going on in the grown-up world and I wasn't really that sure what the protests were about. But I had seen graffiti on the street calling the Minister a dog. Indonesians are usually very polite, even when we disagree. Calling someone a dog is a really, really bad insult.

My friends and I thought the panzers were pretty cool though. My mom, apparently, did not.

That afternoon after school, I was playing in the kindergarten yard with my friend Aris. We weren't in kinder anymore, but there was a cool jungle gym in that yard. It was a big round thing made up of circles, like an open globe with a hole at the very top. It looked like the *Star Wars* Death Star. Back then my head still fit through the smallest circle at the top. But it made me nervous because I was worried that one of these days my head would fit in but not come out. So I was very careful about making sure my head really did still fit going both ways.

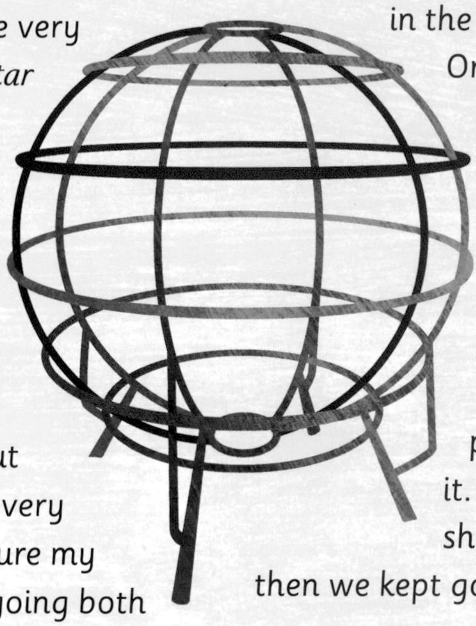

Besides us, the yard was empty because it was late in the afternoon and all the little kids had gone home. We were climbing on the Death Star when someone ran by, yelling, "They're shooting at the university students!"

Aris and I looked at each other. Neither of us had to say anything. We both knew what we had to do. We had to go watch!

It was a hot day and the sun was beating down on the asphalt as we jogged toward the university with our backpacks flapping on our backs. The streets were empty. We didn't want to miss anything, so we picked up our pace. We came upon a poster lying in the middle of the street. On the poster was the image of the Minister with the face of a dog and bloody fangs. Someone with big feet must have stepped on the poster, leaving a boot print that tore through it. I rolled it up and shoved it into my bag, then we kept going.

Suddenly I heard a loud honking from behind us. We turned around, and speeding down the street toward us, horn blaring, was my family's blue station wagon. My mom and two of my uncles were in the car and they were waving and yelling at us. When they pulled up, I could see my mom was upset. "Where do you think you're going? We were looking all over the school for you!"

"We heard they were shooting the university students, so we were going to go and watch," I explained.

It wasn't that it had never occurred to me that my mom would be against it. I knew she didn't like the panzers. And my parents had explained to me some of what was going on and why we needed to be careful these days. They'd told me we had a really mean president. He used to be a general in the military and was used to everyone following his rules. Nobody was allowed to criticize him or his ministers. People who did would end up in jail. Or worse.

I felt like I understood the situation. And I knew what to say and what not to say. But if things were going down, wasn't everyone going to go watch? It only seemed natural.

Apparently my mom didn't think so. Her eyes narrowed to a squint, and she barked, "What!!!?? You heard they were shooting the students and you decided to GO WATCH???"

So. When the military is shooting at university students, and you're a kid, don't go watch. I got that message loud and clear that day.

But it wasn't over for us, because now we were trapped.

***

By heading toward the demonstration, we had made my mom and my uncles drive into an area that the military had then closed off. They were stopping all the cars and checking them for student demonstrators. The problem was, one of my uncles who was in the car with us WAS a university student. He wasn't involved in this demonstration, but if the military saw him, they would think he was a demonstrator trying to escape.

So the grown-ups decided it would be best if nobody saw him. As we approached the checkpoint, he got under a tarp in the back of the station wagon to hide. They let me and Aris hide under the tarp with him. It was totally like we were real secret agents so we lay completely still.

When we got to the checkpoint, my older uncle showed the soldiers his papers. They didn't ask my mom, because they could tell she wasn't a student. Suddenly I heard one of the soldiers say, "Wait. Let me see that yellow bag."

Why was he talking about my school bag? Suddenly, it was like ice ran down my spine. It WAS my school bag that my mom was holding on her lap, and that poster was rolled up in it! Clearly that poster was not allowed. If they thought it was my mom's, or my uncle's, they could get arrested and we'd all be in big trouble!

***

I didn't know what to do.

It was the worst feeling. I knew I had to keep completely quiet and hidden under the tarp, but I felt I was the only one who could explain the poster. Up until then, it had felt like we were playing a game. But now I was scared. It felt like I had a rock in my stomach.

I heard my mom say, "It's just my kid's school bag."

"Where's your kid?" the soldier asked.

My mom had to think fast. "We were just picking the child up, but couldn't get through because of all these blocked roads!"

"So you left your child?"

"No . . . what do you mean?"

"You have the bag but not your child. What's going on here? Sorry, but please give me that bag, *Bu*."

Bu is short for *Ibu*, which is how you refer to a grown-up woman whom you respect, like your mother. But just because he said that, and "sorry" and "please," didn't mean he was being nice. In our culture, the more serious you are, the more polite you sound. I could tell he was getting angry.

My mom on the other hand hadn't grown up in Indonesia. So she had a way of arguing with people that was very un-Indonesian. I knew she was about to say something like

"How dare you take my child's backpack!" She was always protecting me. But this was not going to end well.

Then I heard my uncle laugh. Good, I thought. My uncle will smooth this over.

"Very sorry, sir," he said. "Her kid left the backpack in the car this morning. When we heard there was a demonstration we decided to come in the back way, which clearly was a mistake, since now we're all turned around and we're actually still trying to get to the school. Can you tell us the best way to get back to the school now? Between you and me, these university students are really screwing things up for the rest of us, aren't they? What do they want, anyway? How does making us go in circles to pick up our kids help the country, eh?" He chuckled again.

"Humph," the soldier grunted. "Who knows. Go get that kid. You have to go around. It's pretty late. That child is going to be crying."

He was right about that.

***

Once we were far enough away, my older uncle said, "You can come out now!" I wiped my eyes, and we threw back the tarp. He was chiding my mom. "Next time, it would be better if you just give him the backpack." He was assuming my mother was just being stubborn with the soldier.

"And have them find this?" she said sharply, pulling out the poster with the picture of the Minister as a dog with bloody fangs.

"Woah!" my uncles both gasped. "What's that doing in there? They would have arrested us all!"

All eyes were on me.

I looked at my toes.

My mom explained, "I noticed there was something sticking out of your bag as we were pulling up to the checkpoint. I knew immediately when I started to pull it out."

My uncle added, "If it was just us, we'd probably sit in jail for a day and they'd let us go if we acted sorry enough. But if they figured out who your dad is, they would use it against him. They would say that he was a ringleader, a shadow puppet master behind the protests. They could put him under house arrest. Or worse."

"You really have to be more careful," my mom said, looking straight at me.

We drove home in silence.

masuk
stadiun utama

3

CORRUPTION, COLLUSION, AND NEPOTISM

Putting my whole family in danger was NOT my superpower.

Do you remember the Minister? Well, he had become even more important in the years since I was born. And richer too. Nobody could say so in public, but he got richer because he was *corrupt*. That basically means he used his position of power to steal money.

For example, one time he announced he was going to build a big sports complex. There would be a huge indoor arena for badminton, basketball, and *silat* (which is an Indonesian martial art). There would be outdoor fields for soccer, track, and . . . well, more soccer. Indonesians love playing soccer. And there would be a swimming pool and a diving pool—the works.

The complex was supposed to cost 10 billion *rupiah* and take three years to build. Our tax money was going to be used to pay for it.

Six years later, the country had spent over 20 billion *rupiah*, and the sports complex was still not finished. Of course some of it was there. The soccer field was ready. It wasn't that far from my house, so my friends and I used to ride our bikes down there after school to fly kites. It used to be a swamp, with a lot of poor people's houses made from plastic sheets and cardboard in the open

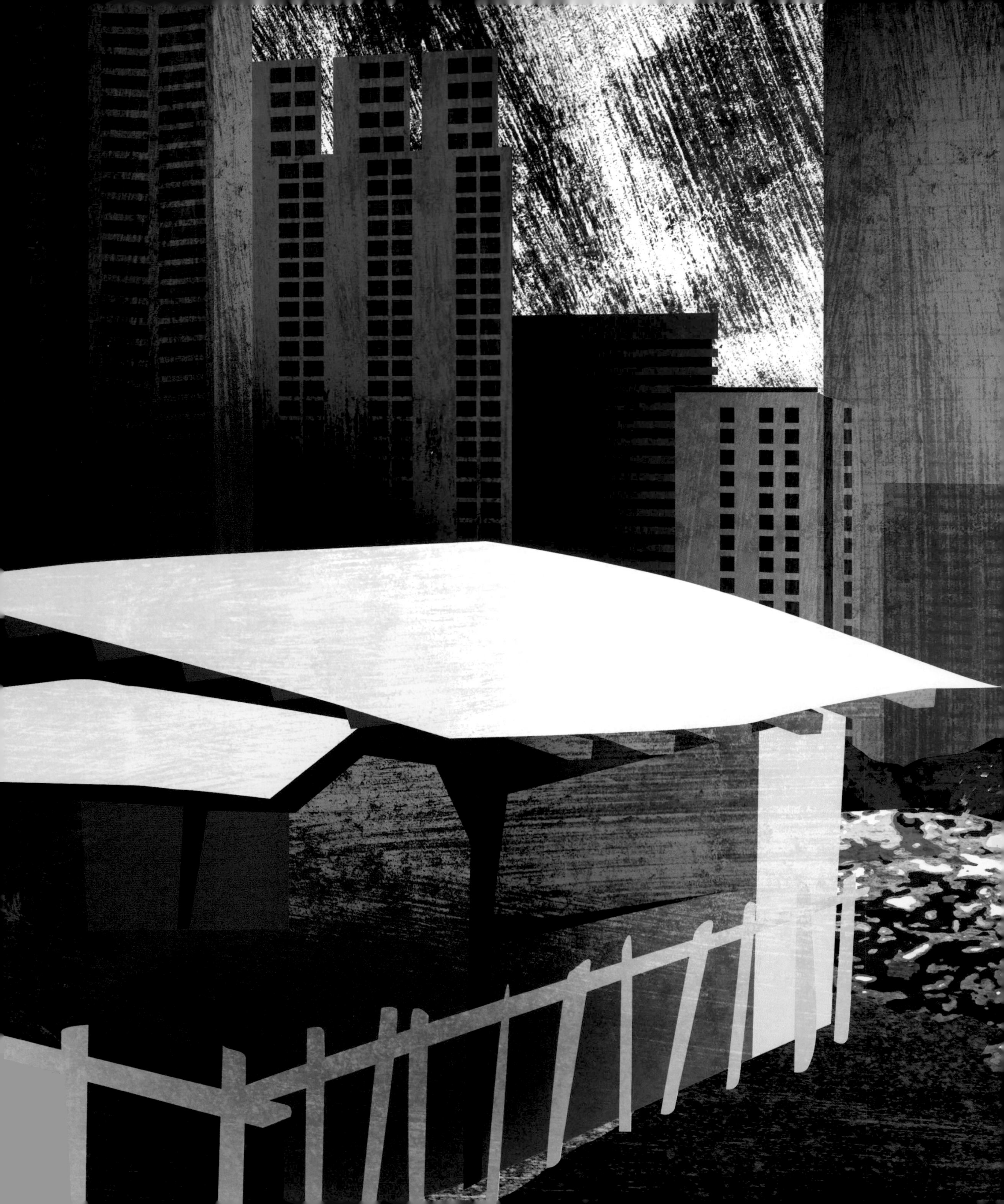

areas around the edge. Whole families who lived there worked as garbage collectors and recyclers. They would head out in the morning pulling big two-wheel carts behind them. They would go from garbage bin to garbage bin, searching for anything salvageable. Or sometimes people would pay them to haul away their garbage. They worked hard all day in the hot sun and still returned home with almost nothing.

Because nobody cared about them, the Minister figured he could take the land for his soccer field. His men went to the garbage collectors and told them they had one week to clear the area. The residents protested, and the Minister got the army to come in and push them out. Anyone who resisted was arrested. Or worse. The army came with bulldozers and bulldozed their houses and put up a tall fence and two goal posts. So now there was a soccer field.

Where did all the money go that was supposed to have been spent on building the sports complex? Well, everyone could guess what had happened. The Minister was suddenly buying expensive cars for his sons and taking his family on trips to Europe and America. He had a big family. Two of his children were grown-ups, two were in college, two in high school, and one was my age. You'll meet Erin soon.

His oldest sons had become very rich after they were given powerful jobs. One of them was the director of the sports complex project. The other was the vice minister for health and sanitation. This is called *nepotism*. It's when a person in power gives jobs to their friends and family instead of to people who actually know how to do the job. Kings and queens used to do this—giving all the important titles to their sons and daughters and close friends. But in a democracy you aren't supposed to use your power to make your family rich and powerful. You're supposed to do what's best for the country.

Corruption and *nepotism* are words you should know. Even in a democracy, when people get into power, they have to be watched. Like my mom always says, "Power corrupts." Even those with the purest intentions will be tempted once they have power. There is something about power that changes you. Maybe you start believing you have power because you alone deserve it. When in fact you are where you are because many people helped you get there. But then those people are no longer around as you surround yourself with people who want to be your friends because they want to be close to power. Those people don't tell you the truth. They always agree with you. They always tell you you're the best. They always say yes and you forget what it's like to hear someone say no to you. And if someone does disagree, you can't even consider that you might be wrong.

To make things worse, those who rise to power are often those who want power and didn't start out with pure intentions. So in a democracy it's important that there be rules to keep those in power from doing whatever they want. Better yet, don't let anyone get too much power to begin with. Power corrupts. Power leads to nepotism.

Besides corruption and nepotism, one other word you should know for this story is *collusion. Collusion* means making secret agreements with someone who's not on your team. It's a kind of cheating. It's hard to know how much the Minister colluded with others because it was all done in secret. But so many things always worked out in his favor that either he was just really, really, really lucky . . . or he cheated. Most likely he was a cheat who colluded with people to get what he wanted.

So corruption is a way the powerful steal to get rich. Collusion is how they make secret agreements to get rich and powerful. And nepotism is how they make their friends and family rich and powerful too. Have you heard of any rich and powerful people in your country doing any of these things?

Well, in Indonesia everyone knew who was doing this. But nobody talked about it in public because they were afraid that if they did they'd get into trouble. This is what is called a public secret.

But things were about to change.

WAR RESISTERS LEAGUE
BLACK PANTHER PARTY
PANTHER POWER
NOW
ORGANIZATION
FOR WOMEN
AMERICAN
INDIAN
MOVEMENT
REMEMBER WOUNDED KNEE
FREE

4

THE OTHER STORM

I mentioned that the real storm was not the monsoon, but a political storm. Revolution was in the air all over the world. There was a lot of news about what was happening in the United States because they had just lost a war in Vietnam. The US president had been forced to resign. Activists from organizations like the Black Panther Party, the American Indian Movement, and the United Farm Workers were fighting for people's rights. A new generation of activists was building the feminist movement, the gay liberation movement, the environmentalist and antinuclear movements . . . It was a time of change.

The rest of the world was on the move too. From Latin America to the Middle East, from Southeast Asia to Europe and Africa, change was in the air. My parents and their friends talked about South Africa and the Soweto uprising. South Africa was another diverse place that, like Indonesia, had been colonized by the Dutch. That history is complicated, and other colonizers like the British also tried to come in and take over. Groups like the Zulu nation had fought back and won. But when I was a kid, the main problem was a small number of white South Africans who had stayed and set up a country where white people had all the rights and black South Africans (and anyone else who wasn't white) were considered second-class citizens. They called this system *apartheid* and it meant separate schools, separate neighborhoods, and separate jobs—with all the good schools, houses, and jobs going to white people only.

So of course people fought back. But when anyone tried to resist, the apartheid government would arrest them. Or worse. The most famous resistance leader from South Africa, whom you have probably heard of, was Nelson Mandela. He spent twenty-seven years in jail for standing up against apartheid.

When I was a kid, Mandela was in jail, and a new generation of younger activists was taking the lead. The Soweto uprising started in the township of Soweto, when the government tried to force black South African kids to speak Afrikaans in school. Afrikaans was the language of the apartheid regime. Everyone else spoke other languages like Zulu and Xhosa at home. So black South African students said no and marched out of school in protest. Twenty thousand students marched out of school! Elementary school students, middle school students, and high

AWAY
WITH
AFRIKAANS

school students. The government sent their police in to stop them with force. Many were hurt. Some were even killed. But the protests didn't stop. The resistance didn't stop. In fact, the resistance continued for many years until the end of apartheid. Eventually, Nelson Mandela would be elected president of South Africa.

At the time nobody knew what would happen. But many people around the world were inspired by the bravery of the South African students.

My parents were the ones who told me the story about the students leading the Soweto uprising. They never told me I had to do that kind of thing. In fact, my father always said, "Whatever you do, don't get arrested! The military here is really mean." But of course I knew he himself just barely escaped getting arrested for one of his books, and many of his friends had been arrested. And I knew my mom had gotten arrested in the United States when she was a student protesting segregation, which was the US version of apartheid. This was something she was proud of, so I felt like I was getting mixed messages.

When my younger brother was born they named him Biko, after Bantu Stephen Biko. Steve Biko was the leader of the Black Consciousness Movement in South Africa, an activist whom a lot of people admired. The apartheid government wanted to blame him for the Soweto uprising and later arrested and killed him. I wasn't sure if I would have wanted to be named after someone who was killed. But my mom said it was just a way to honor Steve Biko and how he inspired people. I said I hoped my brother wasn't inspired to get arrested and killed. My mom had to agree with me on that.

All this activist stuff was kind of interesting, but honestly, for me as a kid it wasn't what I spent most of my time thinking about. I was mostly interested in the same stuff my friends were interested in. Music. Movies. Celebrities. That sort of thing. But all the grown-ups around me were definitely thinking about activist stuff a lot. And talking about it a lot too. They talked about Soweto. They talked about Native Americans occupying Alcatraz Island in California, a revolution in Nicaragua, "troubles" in Ireland . . . And when their voices got more hushed, I could tell they were talking about things right here in Indonesia: about leaders like the Minister, corruption, nepotism, and the brewing storm. When were the people going to get tired of being bullied and rise up? (They always said "THE people," not just "people.") What would be the "spark" that would light the fire? Who were the leaders we could trust?

And then of course there was the epidemic.

5

THE EPIDEMIC

For me, it started with my mom giving me some pills. I don't know if I even asked what they were for. I just took them as instructed. There's a lot of life in the tropics. Which also means there are a lot of germs and parasites. The Dutch colonizers had ruled Indonesia for 350 years and took all our resources without spending any money on the things that you need to make sure that water is clean to drink and food safe to eat. So there were often outbreaks of mosquito-borne diseases like malaria and dengue fever, bacterial infections like cholera and typhoid, and parasites like amoebas and tapeworms. Those of us who could afford it would get our vaccinations and take pills to avoid getting these diseases whenever there was an outbreak. But many people couldn't afford the vaccines and pills. We knew that was unfair, but our family could afford it, so we kept up-to-date on our vaccinations and pills. When my mom gave me some pills to take, I took them without asking questions.

I was in second grade. That day, my tummy was feeling kind of rumbly. It wasn't a stomachache, but I felt really gassy. I was sitting at my desk when suddenly I felt something was wrong in my underwear. I froze. Had I somehow had an "accident"? In second grade?? I was mortified.

PAHLAWAN NASIONAL INDONESIA
UNTUNG SURAPATI 1660-1706
PATTIMURA 1783-1817
DIPONEGORO 1785-1855
MARTHA TIAHAHU 1800-1818
CUT NYAK DHIEN 1850-1908
TEUKU UMAR 1854-1899
AHMAD DAHLAN 1868-1934
CUT NYAK MEUTIA 1870-1910
MARIA WALANDA MARAMIS 1872-1924
SITI WALIDAH 1872-1946
R A KARTINI 1879-1904
COKROAMINOTO 1883-1934
DEWI SARTIKA 1884-1947
TAN MALAKA 1884-1949
KI HAJAR DEWANTARA 1889-1959
FAKHRUDDIN 1890-1929
SAM RATULANGI 1890-1949
RASUNA SAID 1910-1965
ISMAIL MARZUKI 1914-1958
SUPENO 1916-1949
SUDIRMAN 1916-1950
NGURAH RAI 1917-1946
WOLTER MONGINSIDI
PIERRE TEN

I felt something on my left thigh. I looked down, and there it was. A tail. I was growing a tail. It was clearly a tail. It was a bit lighter colored than my skin—kind of almost see-through. But fleshy. Definitely fleshy. And it was attached to me . . . It had to be . . . a tail.

I looked around to see if anyone had noticed. Thankfully, everyone was working on their assignments. My teacher was at her desk, busy writing something. So I slowly put down my pencil. I grabbed my new tail with my left hand and got up. Keeping my tail hidden in my hand, I shuffled up to the teacher.

"My stomach hurts, I really need to go to the bathroom."

She looked up at me. We weren't usually allowed to go to the bathroom during class, but she could tell from my face that making me stay was going to cause problems. Perhaps even the kind of problems someone was going to have to clean up.

"Okay," she said, "but come RIGHT back."

I went slowly to the door, and as soon as I was alone, I ran as fast as I could with one hand holding my tail. When I got to the bathroom, I locked myself in a stall. I let go of my tail, and . . . it fell to the floor. I was confused. It seemed to me like it had to be at least two feet long. It looked like a long white sausage. I had no idea what was going on, so I just squatted there staring at the thing on the floor.

All kinds of thoughts were running through my mind. Was I some sort of mutant devil child? I knew I was different, and being different was a superpower. But did I really want to be THAT different? Like the-kid-with-a-tail kind of different?

I took a closer look at my now detached tail. Okay, it fell off, so maybe it's not a tail. Tails don't fall off. But what is it then? A snake that somehow got into my underwear? A worm? A big worm? Wait. Worm. What did my mom say about those pills she gave me yesterday? Did she say something about worms? Yes. Of course. It was a tapeworm.

Tapeworms are a type of *parasite*—an animal that lives off of another animal. Tapeworms start out as eggs that are too small to see. The eggs get eaten and then hatch in the other animal's stomach. Then they grow by eating the food the host animal eats. In this case, I was the

host animal. And apparently I had been growing a big ol' tapeworm in my gut. It was big enough that I should have named it. Like a pet. The pills my mom gave me must have flushed it out. I was relieved to have figured out what it was, and that was pretty much the end of it for me.

But I was one of the lucky ones. Apparently there was a tapeworm epidemic in Jakarta that year. A lot of money had been given to the Minister to be used for a public health campaign. The Department of Health and Sanitation was run by his son. So all that money was supposed to be spent to help prevent this stuff—tapeworm epidemics. But the money had mysteriously disappeared. No dirty water treatment plants were ever built. And since only people like us who could afford it were getting tapeworm pills, lots of other people were getting really sick with tapeworms.

Some people tried to complain. They organized a demonstration in front of the Minister's office. The organizers had hoped that a lot more people would come out and protest, but most were still too afraid in those days. And for good reason. The police arrested the leaders of the protest and many others had to go into hiding.

The Minister sat watching from his big office window, scowling.

6

BULLIES ON BIKES

One thing about Indonesia is it's diverse. In fact, it's in our national motto: *Bhinneka tunggal ika* (Unity in diversity). Kind of like *E pluribus unum* in the US or *In varietate concordia* in the European Union. The motto comes from a poem written by Mpu Tantular during the reign of King Hayam Wuruk of the Javanese Majapahit Empire in the fourteenth century. It was an important idea as people from all over Indonesia—from seventeen thousand islands and 350 ethnic groups—had come together to fight the Dutch colonizers. Once we won independence, it was clear that we had won because we had united against the Dutch. But now what? Does everyone go back to the days of small kingdoms fighting each other? The answer was no, let's keep this cooperation going and build a diverse nation together.

There are so many different ways of being Indonesian. Take my dad's family, for example. They had a bit of Javanese from Eastern Java. A bit of Madurese from the island of Madura, which is a smaller island off of Java. A bit of Balinese, which is the island most Westerners know about. And even a bit of Bugis, from the island of Sulawesi, which is another big island. I was told the term *boogeyman* comes from Bugis. Dutch colonial ships were terrified of the Bugis. The Bugis are a seafaring people, and when the colonial ships would come to steal spices, the Bugis would raid them. The Dutch called them pirates. My dad called them freedom fighters. I thought it was cool that I was part boogeyman-pirate-freedom fighter.

The Bugis are also cool because they say there are five genders: *makkunrai*, *oroané*, *bissu*, *calabai*, and *calalai*. *Makkunrai* and *oroané* are when you are the gender people think you are when you're born. *Calalai* and *calabai* are when you are a different gender from what people think you are when you're born. And you are *bissu* when you are neither.

Of course one's gender doesn't have to be just one of five options. But five genders are more diverse than two, which is what some people try to insist on. The thing you learn when you grow up in a place as diverse as Indonesia is it's better to keep your mind open.

This isn't to say that everything was always rainbows and unicorns in Indonesia. There were plenty of people who didn't seem to get the idea of celebrating *bhinneka* (diversity). And there was plenty of racism and discrimination.

My classmate Mari was bullied because her family was considered Chinese. Just being called "China" was an insult, even though a lot of Indonesians were of Chinese descent. Just before I was born, many Chinese Indonesians left the country because they were being attacked and persecuted. Those who stayed were treated so badly that many changed their names so they didn't sound Chinese. At home Mari had a Chinese name, but we all knew her as Mari. I actually didn't even know what her Chinese name was.

There was a famous Indonesian activist whose name was Soe Hok Gie, which is a Chinese name. He wrote about political prisoners and corruption even when it was very dangerous to do so. And he refused to change his name. He was also really into mountain climbing. Sadly he died from breathing poisonous gas while climbing the tallest volcano on Java, Mount Semeru. After he died, his writings were published as a book called *Diary of a Demonstrator*. The government didn't officially ban the book, but you knew you weren't supposed to have it. People would make copies of it and share it secretly.

That book would become important to me later.

***

Some rules against Chinese Indonesians were official. Meaning there were actual laws that said stuff like, "Chinese people are not allowed to practice their religion or celebrate the Chinese New Year." Some of these policies started because the Dutch colonizers divided Indonesians up based on race. Chinese people were only allowed to live in certain places and have certain types of jobs. This was a lot like the practices against Chinese people and other people of color in the United States, even after segregation was technically not legal.

But not all our problems came from the Dutch. Some of the laws

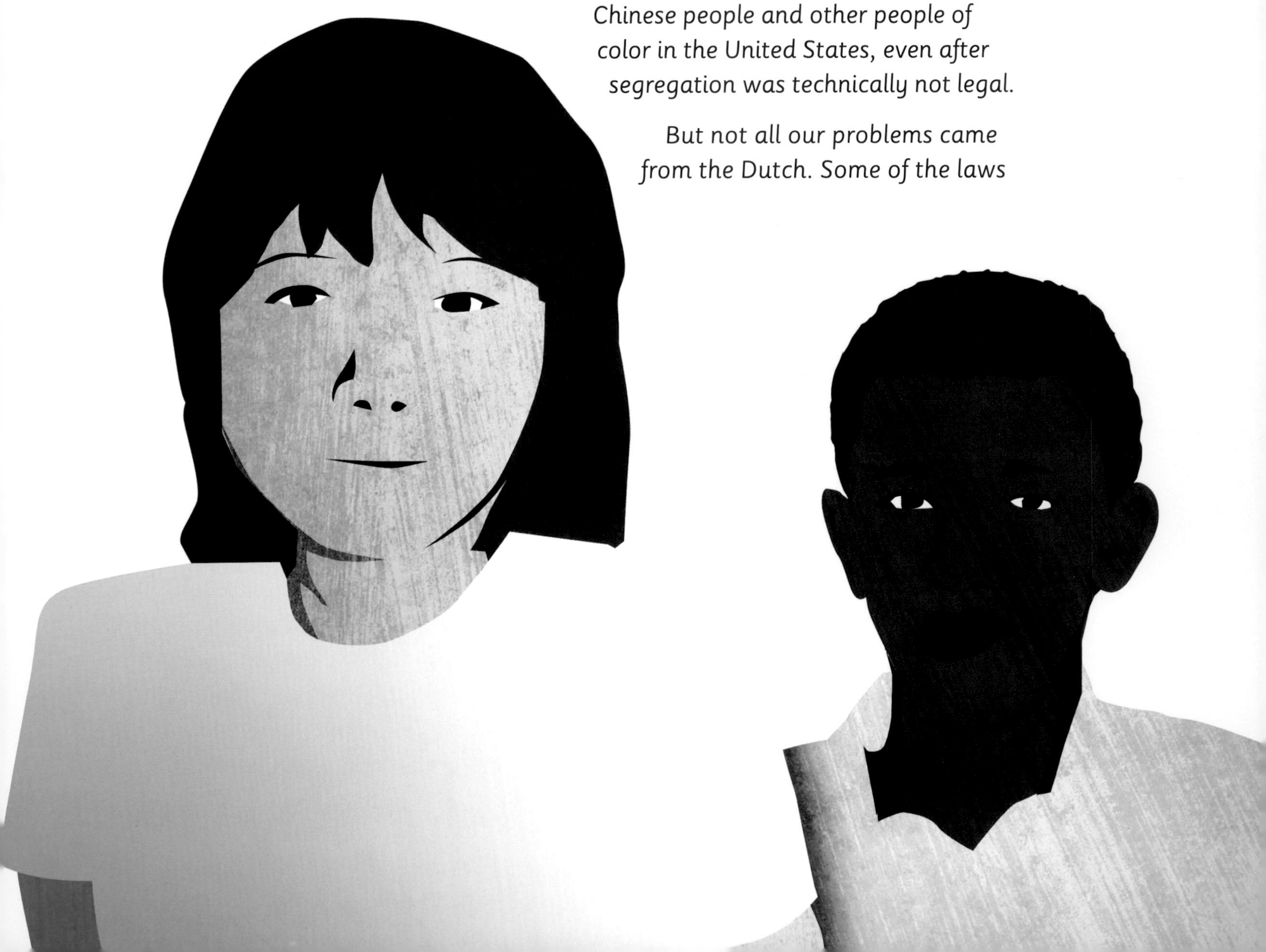

RT.2

7

REVOLUTIONARY VIOLENCE

My aunt Ayu, my father's youngest sister, was a university student and a student activist. Ayu lived with us, so when my parents weren't around, she was the one who'd keep an eye on me. That meant I got to go with her to her activist friends' houses sometimes. They would hang out and play cards or dominoes. There was always a guitar, and they would sing American songs by Joan Baez and Bob Dylan. They'd also sing Indonesian songs by Iwan Fals and Rhoma Irama. And my favorite was when they would sing silly naughty songs with made-up-on-the-spot words that everyone would crack up at. Ayu would pretend to cover my ears.

Ayu and her friends laughed a lot, even about stuff that you'd think they'd be sad about. Like when one of their friends was in jail, they were all joking about how much worse it was going to be for his jailers, since he farted so much. And they could go on for hours. They would say, "You gotta laugh to keep from crying."

They also had serious conversations. My head would be buried in a book—I was a big reader—and they would get deep into serious stuff that they didn't think I was paying attention to.

Like the time her friends Dewi and Faisal got into an argument about what they called "revolutionary violence." Dewi was not a student anymore, and she had just gotten back from six months in Burma, a country north of Indonesia where there was a war going on. She had met a bunch of activists there and one was really close to her. I think maybe they were in love. She had a photograph of the two of them together in the jungle dressed like soldiers that she always kept in her purse. Sadly, her friend was killed in the fighting so she came back to Indonesia.

Faisal was a student at one of the bigger Islamic universities. He was one of the more well-known student leaders at the time, famous for his big smile and rousing speeches.

I tuned in to Faisal saying, "The problem with violence is that even if you win, you've planted a seed that will come back and bite you."

"Maybe," Dewi responded, "but if the generations before us hadn't been willing to take up arms to fight the Dutch, Indonesia wouldn't be free today."

"But that's exactly my point," Faisal said, "we're not free today. We kicked out the Dutch, but now we have a government that only knows the language of violence. I'm not saying we shouldn't have fought the Dutch. But that was a different time and a different enemy. They were an enemy from the outside. Now the problem we have is from within, and we can't plant the same seeds and expect different fruit to grow."

"Who would have thought you were such a pacifist, Faisal," Ayu laughed, to lighten the mood.

"Faisal wants to be the Mahatma Gandhi of Indonesia!" Dewi teased.

Faisal and Dewi both laughed.

Mahatma Gandhi was one of the leaders of the independence movement in India, where they were fighting against the British colonial occupation at the same time we Indonesians were fighting the Dutch. He and his followers were pacifists. They believed that war and violence were wrong even if they might seem to serve your goals. Especially if they might serve your goals. Gandhi's followers used nonviolence and noncooperation to challenge the British. And they won.

"I don't know about that," said Faisal. "But I do know that we have to

be creative, because I just don't see us raising an army and getting freedom that way. I don't think our people want a civil war."

Dewi nodded. "I agree. I'm not suggesting we need a civil war. But look at Martin Luther King in America, he was a pacifist, but would they have paid attention to him if it weren't for Malcolm X? I think the people in power in America figured they had to deal with King or else they would have to deal with someone who wasn't so nonviolent. And even then Martin Luther King was assassinated."

"And so was Malcolm," Faisal added. "No, I get it. This stuff is real and I understand why sometimes it feels like we make it too easy for them to just beat us up and throw our leaders in jail. Or worse. I don't know the answer, but I do know that the military already plants their agents at our demonstrations. They dress up like students and start throwing things. Then they run and hide, and the military uses that as the excuse to shoot at the rest of us. We were all there the last time. They're always looking for an excuse to crack down on us and if we were to start using violence, we'd be giving them that excuse."

"But even if we don't give them the excuse, they make one up, so what's the difference?" Dewi said. "I'd rather not be a sitting duck."

"Me neither, but I think it would just make things worse. But more importantly, I think when we talk about violence it's not just about whether it would work or not. It's about whether it's right or wrong. Who would we kill? It's not like we'd ever get the top commanders. And if we did get the commanders, people would probably just feel sorry for them. They would become martyrs. Realistically it would be foot soldiers who would get hurt. And who are they? Kids from poor families trying to eat." Faisal was starting to get worked up, and when he got worked up he could get pretty preachy. This was great when he was firing up student demonstrators with his speeches. It wasn't such a great way to talk with friends.

And it was clearly not sitting well with Dewi. "You don't have to explain to me who the soldiers are, Faisal. As you know, I have plenty of soldiers in my family. My brother is a marine. I don't want him to die either. But you make it sound like everyone is all innocent," she said. "They'd beat you in a second. Or worse. Some of those guys are total psychos. You said it yourself: these are people who only speak the language of violence."

"Yeah, but I also said it was because that was how they won. I doubt we could win that way anyway, since they have all the weapons. But more importantly, even if we could, then we would become them. Power corrupts. Violence begets violence. Anyway, when's the last time you killed someone? Is that something you really think you could do? Or are you just suggesting other people should do the killing while we cheer them on?"

"I might kill someone today, starting with you!" Dewi said, making an exaggerated mean face with bulging eyes—so everyone knew she was joking.

"I guess I'm not messing with YOU!" laughed Faisal.

"All right you two . . ." said Ayu.

This whole time I was pretending to read my book. The conversation made me think about the bike bullies. How since they were bigger and stronger there had to be more of us to stand up to them. The thing about some people only understanding the language of violence made sense to me. But I also wasn't keen on the idea of Ayu's friends starting a civil war. I didn't mind playing war with my friends, but a real war? Somehow that wasn't going to be good for us kids. I knew that much.

And I still wasn't sure how to apply all this to my other situation.

8

THE LANDSLIDE

My other situation had to do with one of the biggest bullies of all: the Minister himself.

I should probably back up a bit and explain how I got tangled up with the Minister. After all, I was just a kid. But remember, I'm a kid with a superpower. But like most superpowers, what was a strength in one situation could be a weakness in another. I know when most people think about superpowers they think about stuff like being able to fly or lift a car with one hand. That's because they're only thinking about the "power" part and they think that's the same as "strength." But there are also quieter superhero powers, like invisiblity, or being able to hear other people's thoughts. Mine was more like that. Feeling like I was different meant that I was always trying to fit in, while at the same time knowing I'd never really fit in.

So I found myself in a lot of different worlds at the same time. When I was with my friends from Menteng, I was another kampung kid. When I was at school, my teachers saw me as a studious student. When I was at my grandparents' house, I was a devout Muslim. When I was with my aunt

Ayu and her friends, I was a future revolutionary. And when I was hanging out at the Minister's house, I was just a kid who didn't know anything about all that protest stuff.

That's right. I hung out at the Minister's house. The Minister's children went to my school, and his youngest child, Erin, was in my class and was one of my best friends at school. We were in the choir together, and since the Minister had a big house, all of us choir kids would go over there after school to practice. Calling it a "house" is a bit of an understatement. It was more like a mansion. When you entered the living room, there was a real tiger. Really. I swear! It was stuffed of course, but it was still kind of startling to see when you walked into the room. It was posed like it was about to attack, snarling, bearing its big fangs.

The living room was full of big, fancy furniture with lots of carved wood and big glass cabinets full of porcelain dolls and music boxes. We weren't actually allowed to be in the living room. Instead we spent most of our visits out on the very large covered porch, called the veranda.

Erin had everything. A color TV. An electric keyboard. An Atari video game console. And when our class entered the choir competition, the Minister hired a private music teacher so our class would win—which we always did.

The Minister himself was rarely home. When he was home we all sang a little more softly. Once in a while he'd come out and ask, "How's my team doing today?"

Being polite Indonesian kids, we'd say what we were supposed to say: "We have a long way to go, *Om*, we're very sorry we sound so horrible."

Most Indonesian parents would have been encouraging and said something like, "No, no, you all sound great, keep up the good work!"

But he wasn't like that. He'd just grunt and say something like, "Well, you better work harder then. I hope I'm not wasting my money!"

Then he'd leave. We'd look at each other, not sure what to do with that.

Erin would pretend not to be embarrassed.

***

One time I was at choir practice at Erin's house and it started to rain outside. Most of the other kids lived in the neighborhood since we were near the school. As the rain got worse, they decided they had better get home. Since I lived so far from school, I had to wait for my uncle to come pick me up. I was one of the last couple of kids at the Minister's house. We hung out with Erin playing *Space Invaders* on the Atari. As evening came, there was still no sign of my uncle. This wasn't surprising, since big rains often meant flooding, and flooding often meant people were late. The Minister had a phone, but we didn't have a phone at our house so there was nobody to call. This was before cell phones so there really wasn't much else to do but wait. We were used to it.

Erin's mom came out and told us we should come in and eat dinner. I was feeling a bit shy to join them for dinner, but I did as I was told. Dinner was on the table, and as was customary, we all served up and took our plates to the living room to eat while watching TV. Not the fancy front living room with the tiger, but a second living room in the back next to the kitchen, where the smaller TV was. The Minister was there, watching the evening news, and we all joined him.

There had been a deadly landslide that had buried a village in West Java. They were showing the rescue efforts and reporting that the landslide was because the villagers had cut down too many trees around their village. The Minister was shaking his head.

I was sitting cross-legged on the floor in front of the couch eating my dinner when the Minister suddenly took notice of me.

"Your dad is that writer, isn't he?" he asked.

"Mm-hmm," I nodded with my mouth full.

"What does he think about this? He probably thinks it's my fault, doesn't he? He probably thinks if we weren't building that dam, the villagers wouldn't be cutting down the trees above their village. I know he wrote that book about how dams are bad."

It was actually just an article that my dad wrote for a newspaper, not a book. The newspaper that published the article was then banned for a month because of it. I knew better than to correct the Minister though.

Apparently, he was behind a big dam project in West Java, and the village of Cimanji was in the way. I had been to Cimanji with my father when he was doing what he called "research" for the article. The village was in a fertile valley and the villagers grew rice and cassava. I loved going to that village. I was a city kid, and to me the village kids seemed so free. They got to play soccer in the street since there were hardly any cars. The trucks that did drive through the village had to go really slow to avoid getting stuck in the muddy potholes in the unpaved road.

Those kids could pretty much go anywhere, roaming miles from home to go fishing or even hunting sometimes. And though I was a city kid who had nicer clothes and didn't speak Sundanese (the language of West Java), they took me in like we were old friends.

One kid in particular stood out to me. Her name was Kartini. She was named after Raden Adjeng Kartini, an Indonesian National Hero who was famous for advocating for education for girls back in colonial days. That Kartini was a royal princess. My friend Kartini was a village kid. But both were known for being stubborn. Everyone called my friend Tini, for short. She was a really outgoing kid. She was loud. She was always full of questions. She was fearless. Grown-ups would raise an eyebrow when she talked to them because she was so direct with her questions. But she was also super kind and would do anything for a friend.

A gaggle of us kids, led by Tini, would take off for hours while my dad had meetings with the grown-ups. I got to feed goats, chase chickens, and throw rocks at the lizards down by the stream. When I got thirsty, one of the taller kids climbed all the way up a coconut tree and twisted a coconut off and threw it down. Then Tini, who was actually younger than me but was allowed to carry a big machete knife, hacked off the top with four perfect chops. I would have cut off all my fingers, so I was impressed. We drank the sweet, cool milk right out of the coconut. This is a great life, I thought.

But I guess things weren't always so great for those kids. The village had been ordered to move. The dam project was going to flood the valley floor where the village was, to create a huge reservoir. A reservoir is like a big human-made lake, and the water would run through turbines in the dam to generate electricity. Electricity that would then travel through miles and miles of power lines to the big city where I lived. None of the villages would get electricity.

The villagers didn't want to move and had been protesting the order. When my dad and I visited, everyone was hoping that the government would listen. My dad hoped the article he'd written would help. But apparently it didn't, because just two weeks later, the army came in and forced the villagers to move. They were relocated to a new area on the side of a hill above where the reservoir was going to be. The land on that side of the hill was not very fertile and rice wouldn't grow well. Without enough food, they had little choice but to work for the mining company that was hired to break up the rocks to build the dam. Now the villagers had to gather their firewood from the slopes right above their village. Some

cut down the trees whose roots were keeping the soil in place.

Then the monsoons came, and the landslide. And many villagers were killed.

"So somehow he thinks it's my fault, because I made that dam, doesn't he?" the Minister asked again. I hadn't known that it was the Minister who made the dam. But if that was true, he was probably right. My dad probably did think it was the Minister's fault.

But I clearly wasn't supposed to answer that question, so I just stared at my plate. I wanted to find a way to be agreeable, but my superpower was failing me. I couldn't think of anything to say that would let me seem like I was on his side and not betray my dad.

Erin's mom cut in, "Leave the child alone. Kids don't understand this stuff, do you, child?"

"No, ma'am," I said.

But the Minister had to finish his rant. "Remind your dad that those villagers were cutting down trees illegally. Then they come and ask for money when there's a tragedy. Sad. Dams are progress. Our city needs electricity. The dam will make more electricity so you can play Atari with my Erin. Those villagers are standing in the way of progress! They are standing in the way of development! They are unpatriotic! Patriots are going to make Indonesia great again. Most of those villagers you see protesting are probably just paid actors."

That didn't make any sense, even to me as a kid. And I wasn't really listening anyway, because I was thinking about my friend Tini and the other kids I knew from the village . . . wondering if they were okay. Fortunately, the TV news wrapped up, and now it was time for evening cartoons, which the Minister loved. I figured that would be the end of it.

Unfortunately, it wasn't.

9

MY PLAN

Like most bullies, the Minister was a deeply insecure person. And petty. And vengeful. I hadn't even said anything when I was at his house that day, but for some reason, he blamed me for his own outburst. I guess Erin's mom had told him his behavior at dinner toward me was wrong, since I was his guest, and a child no less. But instead of checking himself, he decided I was the problem. Now I was a bad influence and he wanted me out of his kid's school. Meaning my school.

This was a serious problem. Our school was a difficult school to get into because it was considered a very good school. It was a public school where new teaching methods were tried out. I guess we were kind of like lab rats for our teachers. But it also meant we got some of the best teachers in the country, so being a lab rat felt like a good thing. The Minister could have sent his kids to a private school, since he was rich. But instead he sent his kids to our school.

I carpooled an hour each way every day to go to that school, and I'd been going there since kindergarten. Plus, all my friends were there. So I would be pretty bummed if I got kicked out.

My parents were of course furious. They had heard from the principal that the Minister had been asking the school to kick me out because my family was bad for the school's reputation. My parents had to have a bunch of important meetings with our principal.

I felt completely helpless. My parents never blamed me, but somehow I felt responsible. All my friends agreed it wasn't cool. Even Erin seemed a bit uncomfortable but wasn't going to stand up for me. "Sorry, but that's my dad. Too bad your dad is a dissident. My dad always gets his way."

The argument between Ayu, Dewi, and Faisal kept running through my head. My situation wasn't just like theirs. But just like them, I was up against this big bully. I couldn't beat him. I couldn't sweet-talk him. I didn't have a big army to go up against his. So my only option was to be a guerilla fighter and attack his soldiers. Just like Dewi said, the only way powerless people can win is to find a way to turn our weakness into strength. Not to play by their rules. If Erin and I couldn't be at the same school, then I had a solution that was different from the Minister's.

I hatched a plan. I knew my dad had an original copy of the banned book *Diary of a Demonstrator* by Soe Hok Gie hidden behind some of his old theater magazines on the top of his bookshelf. It hadn't moved since I had first discovered it some years back, so I didn't think he'd miss it. I hadn't read it myself, but I knew about it because my aunt Ayu had shown me her photocopy and told me that someday, when I was older, I should really read it. "But don't get caught!" she emphasized.

It was National Heroes Day that Monday, so we had a flag assembly. Flag assemblies in my school were a formal occasion. We all had to wear our marching uniforms, which included a tie and a cap. We marched and stood in the hot morning sun for an hour, singing patriotic songs and listening to speeches and watching the raising of the flag. I hated flag assembly.

But it was the perfect day to hatch my plan. Everyone would be leaving their school bags at their desks to go to assembly. I was going to be the last one out of class and I'd slip the banned book into Erin's school bag. That was my plan. Erin would get caught with a banned book at school. Grown-ups who got caught selling that book could go to jail, I assumed. So at the very least I expected Erin would get expelled. If Erin was no longer a student at my school, then the Minister wouldn't need to kick me out. I was quite pleased with myself for coming up with this plan.

That is, until it seemed to work.

***

At first I didn't think so. I got the book into Erin's bag without getting caught. But then nothing happened. As far as I could tell Erin never noticed it was there. I kept looking over from the other side of the classroom where I sat, and Erin didn't look concerned. The teacher never looked in Erin's bag, so at the end of the day the bell rang and we all went home. To be honest, I forgot about it too and ended up playing marbles all afternoon with Aris.

But the next day, Erin wasn't in class. Or the next. Or the day after that.

I thought getting Erin expelled and beating the Minister at his own game would feel great. Instead, I felt horrible. I kept imagining worse and worse things happening. What if Erin was sent to jail (or worse)? This had been a big mistake. And I didn't know what to do. Do I tell the Minister that I was the one who planted the book? Do I go to my teachers and tell them? Isn't that what a good person would do? Stand up and take responsibility for my actions? But then I might get expelled and that was what the Minister wanted . . . which didn't seem fair either.

So instead I did nothing. Two more days passed with no Erin, and it was eating away at me. I stayed in during recess, trying to read to distract myself. But I ended up just staring at the same page the whole time.

The weekend came around, and I couldn't take it any longer. I had to tell my mom. I waited until she was tucking me into bed.

It was one of those conversations. "Mom, if I tell you something, can you promise not to tell Dad?"

"No."

"Okay, well, can you promise not to be mad?"

"No. But I can promise to be fair. What is it?"

So I told her the whole story. When I was done, my mom sat in silence. Surprisingly, she didn't look that angry. More like she was thinking hard. She finally broke her silence.

"I'm glad you told me. And I'm sorry we haven't really talked about this whole Minister situation with you. That's our fault. But I am troubled that you would do something like this, even to protect yourself. It's not Erin's fault that the Minister is a . . . jerk." (She actually called him something worse, but you get the idea.)

I'd never heard my mom call anyone that before. So that was different.

"And even if it was Erin's fault, you know two wrongs don't make a right, right?"

"I know," I said. "I know now, that is."

"So I do think there need to be consequences. For one thing, you stole our copy of that book, and if this had come out, we could all have gotten into trouble. You know nobody cares if the Minister's kid has that book, but it could be used against your dad if they figured out where it came from."

I hadn't really thought about that. But it seemed obvious when she put it that way. The Minister's family could get away with anything—which was exactly the problem. But wait, didn't Erin get expelled?

"No, the whole family went to Singapore for a week." My mom knew this because the principal had told her. They were going back and forth about whether the school was going to do anything about the Minister's complaint about us. The principal was on our side and told us he was going to try to smooth things over with the Minister. He told us to wait a couple of weeks, since the family was going to Singapore, and hopefully by the time they got back, the Minister would be in a better mood.

My mom did talk to my dad about what I had done, and they decided in the end that my being scared and guilty for a week could count as consequences. That, and I had to actually read *Diary of a Demonstrator* (my parents borrowed Ayu's copy). Which, honestly, was a bit over my head at the time.

Soe Hok Gie wrote a lot about the things he saw in our country during his time and his personal journey to becoming an activist. He was young, but he had read a lot and talked about all kinds of ideas and events that I had never heard of. Some of them were ideas that you weren't allowed to write about at the time. What was interesting though was that not understanding all the ideas didn't keep me from getting a feeling for who he was as a person and why so many people were interested in his book. He wasn't someone who told you what to think. But he was thoughtful and helped you think for yourself. This did have an influence on me later in life.

Erin returned to school the next week, and the Minister seemed to have forgotten about trying to kick me out. I don't know what happened with the book. I couldn't really ask Erin about it without revealing that I was the one who had planted it. But many years later, I wondered if somehow that book did make a difference in Erin's life, given what ended up happening.

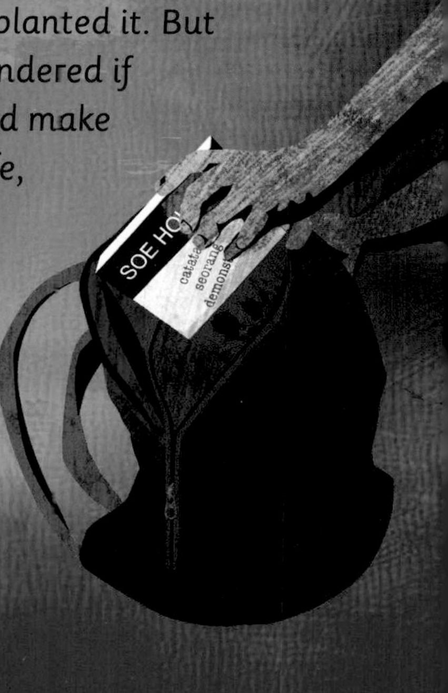

10

HUMANS CAN'T EAT GOLF BALLS

What ended up happening is what this story is really about, you see.

Remember my best friend Sulaiman? After high school, Sulaiman became an environmental activist. Because humans live in the environment too, he was also a human rights activist. He went with other activists to support villagers who were fighting against dams and developments that were taking away their land and benefiting only people in the cities. Dams are bad for the environment. And dams are also bad for villagers. Everyone remembers the Cimanji landslide. But if the villagers complained, they would be put in jail. On the other hand, if city folks said that they were worried about the environment, that was sometimes allowed. Sometimes.

So city activists like Sulaiman would join with villagers who were fighting to protect their villages. Just like when he organized the kids in his kampung to stand up against the bike bullies, Sulaiman now organized with villagers to stand up against rich developers.

In one village, a developer decided to put a golf course in place of the village's rice paddies. The villagers went to the developer and said, "You can't do that. That's land that we need to grow rice to eat." But even though the villagers had been growing rice there for generations, they didn't have papers to show who owned it. So the developer ignored them and the bulldozers came and bulldozed the rice paddies. Armed guards were brought in to keep the villagers away.

So the villagers met to decide what to do about it. They knew if they just went out and took back their land, the armed guards would come and beat them up. Or worse. So they put out a call for *solidarity*—meaning for other people to come and stand with them. Meaning city folks whom the guards might treat less harshly.

Sulaiman and his friends answered the call. And guess who else came? Remember Tini, my childhood friend from Cimanji? Her house was one of the ones that escaped the landslide. But she lost friends and neighbors on that tragic day. She dedicated herself to her studies and went to university, where she became a student leader of the environmental activist group that Sulaiman worked for. They organized university students and other city folks to come and be in solidarity with the villagers. Some of them ended up living in the village for many months.

Tini and Sulaiman were in a meeting about what to do about the golf course. Pak Muchtar was the village head, and he said, "We appreciate you being here. If you weren't here, the developer's thugs would be here every day, making our lives miserable. But because you're here they know people who are connected to the city are watching them.

"However, we still have a problem. Once the rich people start coming here to play golf, it will be impossible for us to get our land back. And I hear they are planning a big opening ceremony and a golf tournament next weekend."

"Hmm . . ." said Sulaiman. "We could get more people here for the weekend and plan to block the road to the golf course."

"I don't know," said Tini, "their armed guards are pretty vicious, and it could turn into a big fight that we may not be able to win."

"And even if we did win that day, then the military would probably come and arrest everyone in the

village," said Pak Muchtar. "We can't take that risk."

It was a familiar conversation if you remember the argument Ayu, Dewi, and Faisal had had many years earlier about what to do when your enemies seem to have more power than you do.

"I have an idea," Tini finally said.

That night, Tini, Sulaiman, and another friend snuck out onto the golf course. They were all student activists from the city. They knew if they got caught it would be bad for them, but it would be much, much worse for any of the villagers.

There were guards at the front gate, but it was a big golf course and the villagers showed them how to get around to the back through the forest. The forest at night was loud with the songs of frogs and the buzz of insects. The four activists made their way to the edge of the golf course and crawled under the barbed wire fence. They didn't know anything about golf, but they figured the places where there were flags near holes must be important.

They found one big area of green grass with a hole with a flag in the middle, and they started to dig. They dug huge letters into the grass. The letters spelled out "HUMANS CAN'T EAT GOLF BALLS." Then they snuck back out through the forest.

Golf courses have to be smooth with short grass, so the developer was furious. It took them a week to fill in the holes and grow the grass back. Meanwhile, nobody could play golf so the opening was put off for two weeks.

Then, the night before the course reopened, the activists struck again. This time they spelled out "RICE IS LIFE. GOLF IS BORING." This happened over and over. The developer sent his guards to the village to find out who had done it. They questioned the villagers rudely, but nobody told them anything. They tried posting guards at night, but it was a big golf course, so the activists always found a way.

In the end, since the golf course could never be used, the developers abandoned it, and the villagers reclaimed their land.

11

NO GOLF FOR YOU TODAY

The villagers getting their land back was good for them, of course. But it was also an important event for other people whose land had been taken from them all across our country. Newspapers and television stations weren't allowed to report on the villagers' success in fighting the golf course. But the story spread anyway, and other villages whose land had been taken away decided to stand up and fight back. The story spread by word of mouth. The story spread through underground newspapers. The story spread through the Internet, which was still new at that time. And the story spread through music and song.

One of those songs was written by Awan. Awan, if you remember, was the kid who got bullied a lot because he wasn't "boy" enough.

And yet Awan had become a famous singer in a pop band called Greenhouse. His stage name was Awan Tru, because he was known for speaking the truth. A lot of his songs were love songs. Some of his songs were about nature and beauty. But his most popular songs were laments—songs about the suffering of people who are poor and mistreated in love and in life. His words were really poetic and sometimes hard to understand. They seem to be about *nasib*—the fate that befalls you:

Why must it be
must it be, must it be
my burden to bear
Why must it be
It must be

The sins of my father
my mother's mistakes

Time and time again
my people betrayed
But today it is me
it is me, it must be

my sadness to share
my own burden to bear

While you play golf today
While you play golf today

Maybe the songs were personal for him and really were about the pain of being bullied every day. Speaking his truth was his way of not letting the bullies win. Later in the song, the lament turns into a fight song:

Mister Big Shot
you must be
must you be afraid
now they rise, now we rise
now I rise

Did you think all would be
always be
yours to have, yours to take
yours to steal

In the streets
now they rise, now we rise
now I rise

It's too late to say
Goodbye. Good day
I'm sorry to say

No golf for you today
No golf for you today

And now the song took on a new meaning. Everyone believed it was really about the country. The downtrodden person in the song represented all poor people, and "Mister Big Shot" must be a corrupt minister—or even the president! A song that said the president was a bully would be banned immediately of course. But Awan's songs were clever. By the time the government censors figured out what people were saying the songs were about and tried to ban them, it was too late. The songs were playing all over the radio. Awan Tru concerts were packed. And everyone knew the words when he got up and sang through a bullhorn at what became the biggest protest in Indonesian history.

But we'll get to that.

12

REFORMASI

That was when things started to reach what some people call the "Tipping Point." There's a story that activists like to tell, called "The Parable of the Hundredth Monkey." According to the story, scientists in Japan were studying macaque monkeys. There were thousands of monkeys. But the researchers saw that one monkey figured out how to wash a potato before eating it. It was so much better that way. Then another monkey saw the first one and tried washing its potato, and also liked it better. And then another monkey learned to wash its potato from the first two. And so on, until ninety-nine monkeys learned to wash their potatoes from each other. But when the next monkey, the one hundredth monkey, learned how to wash its potato, suddenly something amazing happened. From then on all the thousands of macaque monkeys washed their potatoes.

Activists like to tell this story because it's about how sometimes you try, and you try, and you try, and maybe you almost give up because you don't feel like you're getting anywhere. And then, suddenly you realize that you're winning. When just a few people do something, it seems unusual. Even if ninety-nine people join, it still seems impossible because there are still nine hundred and one people who didn't. But when you hit that Tipping Point—in the parable one hundred is the magic number—suddenly it becomes what everyone does from then on.

Reformasi was the name people used when talking about the movement that formed around this Tipping Point in Indonesia. *Reformasi* means "reform." To re-form means to form again, or to reshape. It doesn't necessarily mean to get rid of or start all over again. But it means to take what we have that isn't working and shape it into something that does work for everyone.

Reformasi was a *movement*, because it was a time when many different people came together and started "moving" toward the same goals. The most famous goals were to end what everyone was calling KKN. KKN stood for *Korupsi*, *Kolusi*, and *Nepotisme*. That's Indonesian for corruption, collusion, and nepotism: the things that had enriched the Minister and his family. The reason why so many regular Indonesians were still poor.

But the Reformasi movement was really about more than reform, and it started many years before it had a name. It started with really brave activists who were far ahead of their time. People like Dewi and Faisal and my aunt Ayu who were student activists when I was a kid. Students who came out and protested even when the military would come in with their panzers.

Dewi, Faisal, and Ayu were no longer students by the time the Reformasi movement came together. And they never did try to start an armed revolution. Dewi worked for an organization that defended workers' rights. She was a union organizer. Faisal worked for an organization that defended journalists when they were attacked for trying to tell the truth. My aunt Ayu became a teacher at the university. Each in their own way was trying to change the world. Fighting for workers' rights, defending journalists, and teaching the next generation of students were how they made a difference.

Then came a new generation—activists like Tini, Sulaiman, Pak Muchtar, and the villagers who fought against the golf course. It was risky, and they knew if they got caught it would be bad news. But they were united and had each other's backs.

Maia and Erin ended up going to the same university. They were both involved in student leadership—mostly leading campus activities like organizing volunteer days and planning graduation ceremonies. That is, until the Reformasi movement.

Students were rising up and speaking out about corruption, collusion, and nepotism. One student of course knew about this better than anyone. As a student leader, Erin was often asked to speak at assemblies. This time instead of just saying, "My dad always wins," Erin stood up and said, "I know my father is corrupt, but I'm standing with the rest of you!" Then Maia and the other student leaders called on other students to join the movement.

And the movement grew. Across the country environmentalists and villagers came together with workers and human rights activists. Journalists came out along with teachers and artists. Religious leaders and city workers were arm in arm in the streets. There were banners everywhere saying "NO KKN!"

Many different people started coming to the protests, and the movement began to reach that Tipping Point. Paulus, my friend whose family was from Ambon, joined a march led by doctors. He had become a doctor and was very involved in trying to stop health crises like the tapeworm epidemic.

My friend Mari also got involved even though it was especially dangerous for her as a Chinese Indonesian woman. She had gotten a job working for a travel agency. She didn't consider herself an activist. But she organized her office to donate food to the students when they all marched out of their campuses and occupied the parliament building.

***

The parliament building was the meeting place for the government. It was where all the ministers went to make their decisions about how to run the country. It was built back in the 1960s and no other building looked like it. The roof was two curved arches, designed to look like the wings of the Garuda bird, Indonesia's national symbol.

Protests and marches had been going on for weeks. Each time, the military would come out and stop the marchers, surround them, and force them back to where they started. The next day, a different group would come out and try again. It was a dangerous time for many.

Remember how when I was a kid I went to try to see the demonstration near my school? Now I was a newspaper reporter, and taking photos of demonstrations was my job.

Then it happened.

I was on my way to take photos of a protest in front of Trisakti University. Traffic was really bad in Jakarta, especially on protest days, and I was on the bus. Suddenly all the traffic stopped and there were people everywhere running between cars in the opposite direction. I leaned out the window and asked them, "What's going on?"

"They're shooting at the university students!" one person yelled as they ran past my bus.

Suddenly I was transported back to my school playground again. But instead of excitement, I felt my heart drop. I knew I should go take photos of what was happening. I'd seen some tough things as a photographer. But did I really want to see this? This would be real, not a movie. And what good would my photos do? The government probably wouldn't allow them to be published anyway. But wasn't it my job to document this? If nobody was willing to bear witness to what happened, wouldn't that make it worse? I realized how ironic it was that when I was a kid I really wanted to see something like this but wasn't allowed to, yet now that it was my job to bear witness I no longer wanted to.

I took a deep breath, threw my camera bag over my shoulder, and got off the bus. Most people had stopped running, and traffic was at a standstill. I pulled out my press badge and put it on. The press badge was basically a big plastic card that said "PRESS" that I hung around my neck. The idea was to let everyone know I was a neutral reporter, and I wasn't taking sides. In theory, the authorities wouldn't arrest me for doing my job. That could backfire of course if they really didn't want the press to see what they were doing. Then they could be looking to stop reporters. You never really know, but that day I chose to play by the rules. If they stopped me, then that would be on them. And hopefully I'd be less likely to get shot myself. I really was not liking my job at that moment.

I made my way through all the stopped cars to the side of the road and headed up toward the overpass that looked out on the university. I figured I could get a good view from there without being in the line of fire. But I didn't get far. Ahead, three panzers were blocking the road and the overpass was swarming with military, police, and the feared "Brimob" mobile brigades. It was eerily quiet. If there had been

shooting, it had stopped. A crowd was beginning to gather at the bottom of the overpass to see what had happened. The military was not letting anyone through, especially not reporters. I approached the guy who looked like he was in charge, held up my press badge, and asked what was going on.

He told me to get lost. Well, actually he told me he was going to turn around, and if I was still there when he turned back, I'd be finished. He didn't say what he meant by "finished," but I decided not to stick around to find out.

So I didn't get any useful photos that day.

They weren't able to keep what happened a secret though. To this day, we still don't know who gave the order, but basically, the soldiers had opened fire on the demonstration. Many were injured, and four university students were killed.

That was the Tipping Point. In protest, eighty thousand students marched out of class to the parliament building and occupied it. There were so many students that they couldn't all fit inside. They said they would not leave, and the government would not be allowed to operate until things changed. Outside, even more people gathered to support the students. At this point, even some soldiers decided they had to switch sides. I know this because Aris, my friend from third grade, was in the army now. He was from a poor family and he couldn't afford to go to college. So he joined the army after high school because they would pay for his education. He told me later he wasn't keen on the protesters, but he remembered that time we went to go watch the army shooting the university students when we were kids. And he knew now that even though he had joined the army, he never wanted to be one of those soldiers who was shooting at his own people.

The students occupied the parliament building for days. Supporters brought them food and supplies. Eighty thousand students was a lot of mouths to feed! The military agreed to let the students stay while they negotiated with the government.

When the president realized that the military was no longer willing to crack down on the protests he knew he had lost.

So on the *fifth* day of the student takeover of parliament, the president resigned.

***

This was the end of a regime that had been in power for THIRTY-TWO years—my whole life! This was the biggest change for me since that day thirty-two years ago when I let out my first howl into the eye of a monsoon storm.

Now, there were many more howls.

For many, they were howls of celebration. When the students who were occupying the Parliament building heard the news, their cheers could be heard across the city.

Environmentalists celebrated. Workers celebrated. Villagers celebrated. Garbage collectors celebrated. This was a chance for a new beginning.

It was like a heavy blanket had been lifted. In town squares people were setting up stages to have public debates about how the government should be run. Just a month earlier, that would have been shut down in no time flat. But now people felt they could say things they weren't allowed to say before.

For my family, like for many others, it was personal. My father's

banned articles could now be published as a book. He went on to write many more books without the fear of being banned. Some were even bestsellers.

But amid all this celebration there were also howls of anguish. Those who supported the regime didn't just roll over and disappear. They weren't going to give up their power that easily. Chaos was orchestrated from the shadows. In some places there were riots where many people were hurt. In other places there was fighting that ended up lasting for years. Yet again Chinese Indonesians were attacked and many felt they had to leave the country for their safety. Mari was okay, but she was one of those who left because she didn't feel safe.

But that's not my story to tell. It's one that continues to be written today.

***

I think this is when I really grasped that being different could be a strength. That not fitting in was my superpower. All those years of trying to "fit in" meant I was always searching for what was truly me—what was "authentically" me. But I was doing that by trying to fit in with other people, and I always felt like I was kind of a fake.

It turns out a lot of kids feel that way. In fact, it turns out a lot of

grown-ups feel that way too. That feeling has never gone away for me. But I came to accept that what was always a struggle was also a strength. I had the ability to have friends from many different backgrounds. Rich and poor. Activist and military. Young and old. I could be friends with them because I could see myself in all of them. It's not that I got along with everybody all the time. But if I wanted to get along with someone, I usually could.

This really helped me in my newspaper reporter job, because I could talk to almost anyone and get almost anyone to talk to me. I wanted the articles I wrote to be useful. I tried to answer questions like, who gave the orders to shoot the Trisakti students? Who had been stealing our people's money through corruption, collusion, and nepotism? Because of my ability to put myself in other people's shoes, I could get them to tell me things. Some of these people were so used to being in power, and so used to getting away with everything, they would tell me about the ways they abused their power. They thought I would be impressed. And I was.

But I would write my articles honestly, leaving out no details. There was a new commission investigating corruption, collusion, and nepotism. The commission often used my articles as evidence in trials of corrupt officials. Some officials were fired. Some even went to jail.

And guess who ended up getting in deep trouble with the KKN commission?

That's right. About a year after the president resigned, the Minister himself was arrested, and eventually convicted, for stealing The People's money through corruption, collusion, and nepotism.

THE END

EPILOGUE

M IS FOR MOVEMENT

Every social movement is different. How change happens is going to be different in different places and at different times. There is no single formula for how to build a movement. My story is set in Indonesia in the not-too-distant past. You're probably growing up in a very different time and place. But I share this story because too often there's only one story that's told: the story of the single perfect, honest, confident, strong, smart, brave, always-sure-of-themselves superhero of a person who always does what is right and inspires others to join them, and thus an unstoppable movement is born and we win.

There's nothing wrong with trying to be the best you can be, or being inspired by exceptional leaders. But superheroes aren't real. It's real people who make real social change movements a reality. Real social change movements need all kinds of people, with all their superpowers.

Real social change movements need people who are willing to fail, because movements need people who try even when it seems unlikely that they will succeed. And real social movements need other people who can't afford to fail, because the stakes are real.

Real social movements require people who are impatient, because the time will only ever be right if you make it right now. And real social movements require people who are patient, because change can sometimes take a very long time.

Real social movements need people who are loyal and united, because it takes trust to take risks together. And real social movements need people who are willing to disagree, and people who are willing to change their minds.

Real social movements need people who are stubborn, because change requires persistence. And real movements need people who are flexible, because we learn through listening and recognizing when we are wrong.

Remember what I said in the beginning about my story not being exactly a true story? Well, I hope you understand what I mean now. There is not just one way for something to be true. In fact, sometimes two things that seem like they can't both be true at the same time, have to be. Strengths can be weaknesses and weaknesses can be strengths. For social change movements to succeed, ideas that seem like opposites are often necessary companions.

"We shouldn't be looking for heroes. We should be looking for good ideas."

—Noam Chomsky

DEDICATED TO ARIEF ROMERO AND HIS MAMA, KRISTI

Thank you *first* and *foremost* all the kids and their *families* who read and listened to my *drafts* and gave me your *feedback*: *Arief*, Thea, Bridger, Haraldur, Hugo, Lucia, Marcos, Eva, Helen, Oliver, Paloma, Sadie, Andie, Joaquin, Nico, Yuji, Camilo, Dezi, Augie, Emma, Sacha, Asher, Aiko, Ena, Emma, Theo, Silar, Ila, Kavi, Arlo, Crestmont School in Richmond *Griffin* Class *of* 2019, Center *for* Early Education Class *of* 2019. You're the reason I write.

It takes a community *for* a book to come to *life* and I have so many people to thank. Thank you Kristi *for* always supporting me. Thank you my Orchard communty *for* creating the space. Thank you Gung Ayu and Maya Christina Gonzalez *for* your lived experience. Many thanks to Biko Nagara *for* your help with "Awan's Song." Thank you also Cholil Mahmud, Irma Hidayana, and my *Efek* Rumah Kaca *friends for* your musical insights and inspiration. Thank you Design Action Collective *for* allowing the time. Thank you my Bay Area children's book community *for* all the support.Thank you Dan Simon *for* your trust and collaboration and so much more. Thank you the rest *of* the crew at Seven Stories Press/Triangle Square Books *for* Young Readers *for* your expertise.

Children's book author and illustrator INNOSANTO NAGARA's books encourage children to grow up with confidence in themselves, and to be proactive citizens who are passionate about causes from environmental issues to LGBTQ rights and civil rights. Born and raised in Indonesia, Inno moved to the US in 1988. After studying zoology and philosophy at UC Davis, Inno moved to the San Francisco Bay Area, working as a graphic designer for a range of social change organizations before founding the Design Action Collective, a worker-owned cooperative design studio. Inno lives in Oakland in a cohousing community with nine adults and eight kids.

Inno's first book, *A is for Activist*, started a movement in social justice book publishing for children. After it came *Counting on Community*, then *My Night in the Planetarium* and *The Wedding Portrait*. *M is for Movement* is the fifth title written and illustrated by Innosanto Nagara.

Inno's books stand in solidarity with people of all ages, races, gender identifications, and backgrounds. They suggest that your family isn't only yourself and your parents but also the community in which you live, the histories of those around you, and the natural environment on which we depend for our food and water and air. The ideas in Inno's books may sometimes sound controversial, but they speak to us in a language that is pure common sense and in tune with our natural wishes and inclinations as human beings.

A Triangle Square Books for Young Readers edition, published by Seven Stories Press

Seven Stories Press
140 Watts Street
New York, NY 10013
www.sevenstories.com

Library of Congress Cataloging-in-Publication Data

Names: Nagara, Innosanto, author, illustrator.
Title: M is for movement / Innosanto Nagara.
Description: First edition. | New York : Seven Stories Press, [2019]
Identifiers: LCCN 2019010211| ISBN 9781609809355 (hardback) | ISBN 9781609809362 (ebook)
Subjects: LCSH: Revolutions--Indonesia--Juvenile literature. | Social movements--Indonesia--Juvenile literature. | BISAC: JUVENILE FICTION / Social Issues / General (see also headings under Family).
Classification: LCC HM876 .N34 2019 | DDC 303.48/4--dc23
LC record available at https://lccn.loc.gov/2019010211

Printed in China.

9 8 7 6 5 4 3 2 1

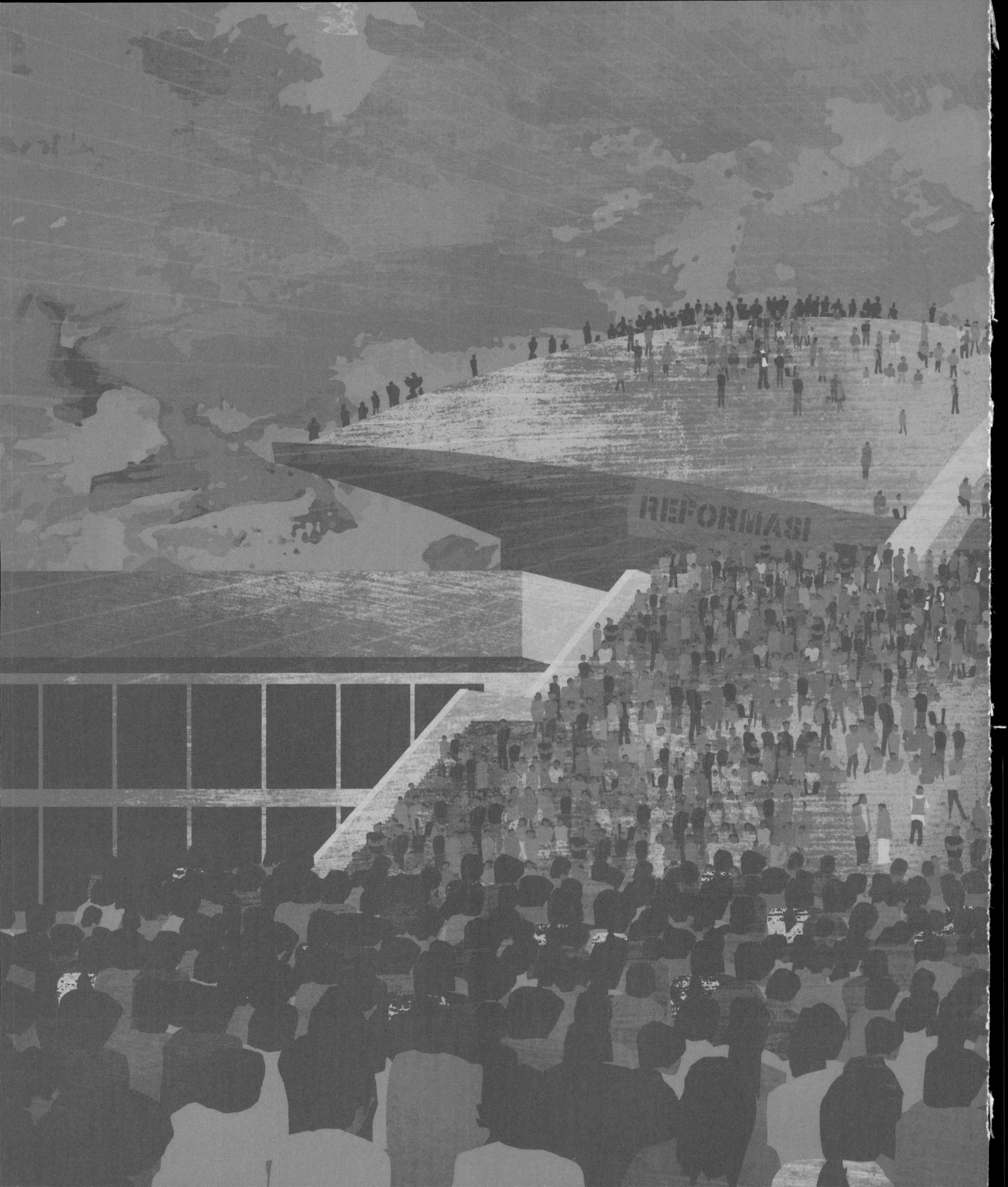
REFORMASI